This Little Tiger
book belongs to:

Mara Alperin

Illustrated by
Miriam Latimer

The Gingerbread Man

LITTLE TIGER PRESS
London

Mr and Mrs Baker lived all alone. Day after day, they baked big gooey cakes, sweet crumbly pies and piping hot pastries. But they had no one to share them with, and that made them very sad.

Then one day, Mrs Baker made a little gingerbread man
to cheer them both up. He had jolly jelly buttons
and a big icing smile. Dusting the flour from her hands,
she popped him into the oven . . .

But to Mr and Mrs Baker's surprise, when the tray came out, the gingerbread man leaped up onto the table, and began skipping through the sugar!

"Tee hee hee! You can't catch me!" he giggled.

"Bless my cinnamon stars!" cried Mrs Baker as they chased him over pots, under pans and all around the kitchen . . .

But the gingerbread man was too quick for them, and he **jumped** right out of the window!

Scurrying along the path,
the gingerbread man ran into
a **very hungry** cow.
"You look tasty," mooed
the cow. "And what fine jelly
buttons you have!"

But the gingerbread man just
danced and pranced, singing,

"Run, run, run,
As fast as you can,
You can't catch me,
I'm the gingerbread man!"

And off he ran – as fast as his
gingerbread legs could carry him!

With a great Mooo! the cow thundered
after the gingerbread man,
past the milk churns,

through the barn,

and round and round
the haystack, until . . .

CRASH!

The haystack tumbled over,
right on top of
the cow!

"Oh, milkshakes!" cried the
very dizzy cow.

The gingerbread man scampered up the hill.
At the top was a **very hungry** goat.
"Good day," bleated the goat.
"I **love** munching thistles, but **you**
look even **better** to **eat**."

But the gingerbread man just whirled and twirled, singing,

"Run, run, run,
As fast as you can,
You can't catch me,
I'm the gingerbread man!"

And off he whizzed – leaving a trail of gingerbread crumbs behind him!

So the goat dashed after the gingerbread man, through the thistles,

over the gate,

and in and out of the apple orchard, until . . .

SMASH!

The goat butted right
into a tree and the
apples came
toppling
down
with a

thud!

thud!
thud!

"Oh, nettles!" cried the goat,
rubbing his head.

"Tee hee hee," laughed the gingerbread man, as he frolicked through the meadow. There, dozing in a tree, was a **very hungry** cat.

"Hello," miaowed the cat. "You look like the **purr-fect** snack!"

But the gingerbread man just
wiggled and giggled, singing,

"Run, run, run,
As fast as you can,
You can't catch me,
I'm the gingerbread man!"

And off he whooshed – racing down
the lane!

Licking her lips, the cat chased the
gingerbread man, around the bush,

through the daisies,
and towards the pond.

The cat pounced up, up, up...

and came down,
down,
down...
SPLASH!

right in the middle of the cold, wet pond!

"Oh, whiskers!" grumbled the very soggy cat.

As the gingerbread man
ran down the hill, he began
to laugh and sing,

"Tee hee hee, I'm having fun,
I've run away from everyone!
A curly-haired woman,
A man in a hat,
A cow and a goat,
And a silly, old cat!"

But when the gingerbread man reached
the riverbank, he stopped and shivered.

"Brrr, too cold! How
do I cross?"

Just then, a fox appeared.
"Hello, little gingerbread man,"
he grinned. "Perhaps I can help you?
Just climb on my tail and I'll
carry you across."

"**Brrr, too chilly!**" the gingerbread man squealed, as the fox paddled into the river.

"Then why don't you climb onto my back?" asked the fox.

"**Brrr, too wet!**" squeaked the gingerbread man, as the water swirled at his feet.

"Climb onto my head," smirked the fox, and the gingerbread man scrambled up.

But the water rose higher still, so the gingerbread man climbed to the top of the fox's nose.

"Tee hee hee! They'll never catch me!"

he cried, just as ...

...the fox tossed the gingerbread man up, up, up in the air and opened his mouth wide...

SNAP!

And that was the end of the gingerbread man!

"Oh dear," sighed Mrs Baker. "What a naughty gingerbread man he was."

"I'm still hungry!" mooed the cow.

"Me too-oo," bleated the goat.

"So am I," miaowed the cat.

Then Mr Baker said, "Let's all go and bake something else together!"

So they all trotted back to the bakery to mix and stir cakes and pastries and pies ... but no more gingerbread men! It was a **fantastic feast**, and with their three new friends, Mr and Mrs Baker were **never** lonely again!

My First Fairy Tales

are familiar, fun and friendly stories – with a marvellously modern twist!

Little Red Riding Hood

The Three Billy Goats Gruff

Jack and the Beanstalk

Goldilocks and the Three Bears

The Gingerbread Man

The Three Little Pigs

Chicken Licken

Rumpelstiltskin

Pssst! coming soon!

The Elves and the Shoemaker

The Ugly Duckling